To the hungry people of the world—PETE AND PAUL

For Judy—MICHAEL

Music and Lyrics by Pete Seeger, David Bernz,
Paul DuBois Jacobs and Jennifer Swender

G. P. PUTNAM'S SONS
A division of Penguin Young Readers Group
Published by The Penguin Group
Penguin Group (USA) Inc., 375 Hudson Street, New York, NY 10014, U.S.A.

Penguin Group (Canada), 10 Alcorn Avenue, Toronto, Ontario, Canada M4V 3B2 (a division of Pearson Penguin Canada Inc.) Penguin Books Ltd, 80 Strand, London WC2R 0RL, England. Penguin Ireland, 25 St. Stephen's Green, Dublin 2, Ireland (a division of Penguin Books Ltd.) Penguin Group (Australia), 250 Camberwell Road, Camberwell, Victoria 3124, Australia (a division of Pearson Australia Group Pty Ltd). Penguin Books India Pvt Ltd, 11 Community Centre, Panchsheel Park, New Delhi - 110 017, India. Penguin Group (NZ), Cnr Airborne and Rosedale Roads, Albany, Auckland 1310, New Zealand (a division of Pearson New Zealand Ltd). Penguin Books (South Africa) (Pty) Ltd, 24 Sturdee Avenue, Rosebank, Johannesburg 2196, South Africa. Penguin Books Ltd, Registered Offices: 80 Strand, London WC2R 0RL, England.

 Published simultaneously in Canada. Manufactured in China by South China Printing Co. Ltd. Design by Cecilia Yung and Gunta Alexander. Text set in Stone Serif Medium.
The illustrations are rendered in acrylics on gessoed linen canvas.

Library of Congress Cataloging-in-Publication Data
Seeger, Pete, 1919– Some friends to feed: the story of Stone Soup / by Pete Seeger and Paul DuBois Jacobs; illustrations by Michael Hays.
p. cm. Summary: A poor but clever traveler finds a way to get the townspeople to share their food with him in this retelling of a classic tale, set in Germany at the end of the Thirty Years War. [1. Folklore.] I. Jacobs, Paul DuBois. II. Hays, Michael, 1956– ill. III. Title.
PZ8.1.S453So 2005 398.2'0944'02—dc22 2004020474 ISBN 0-399-24017-9
1 3 5 7 9 10 8 6 4 2
First Impression

Some Friends to Feed

The Story of Stone Soup

Pete Seeger • Paul DuBois Jacobs

Illustrated by Michael Hays

G. P. Putnam's Sons • New York

A long, long time ago, there was a war. And after the war, there was a famine. That means there wasn't enough food for anyone.

Imagine not eating for one day.

Imagine not eating for three days.

Well, early one morning, a soldier making his way home came to a small village. He hadn't eaten in *five* days!

He asked for food at the first house he saw.

"*You're* hungry?" said the farmer's wife. "This whole village is hungry! Soldiers have robbed us of everything."

Slam!

"*Food!?*" growled the blacksmith. "We're so hungry, we're eating grass."

"Only animals eat grass," said the soldier.

"Well, we can't very well eat stones, can we?"

Slam!

The soldier walked away hungry, but the blacksmith had given him an idea. At the village well, the soldier asked, "Who wants to make some Stone Soup?"

The villagers thought he was joking. "A soup from stones?"

"Of course," said the soldier. "Stone Soup is delicious!"

"Until the stones break your teeth," sneered a woman washing clothes.

But the children were curious.

“How do you make Stone Soup?” the youngest girl asked.

"First, we need the biggest pot you can find," said the soldier. Together, the children rolled out a huge pot.

“What does Stone Soup taste like?” the youngest boy asked.

“That depends,” said the soldier. “What kind of stones do you have around here?”

The children dashed off and came back with some stones.
“This one is too bumpy,” said the soldier.

"That one is too long and thin. But these smooth, roundish stones are perfect."

"Playing tricks on children," grumbled the grown-ups.

The children filled the pot with water. The soldier built a fire. He washed the stones and added them one at a time.

"Mmmm! This stone looks particularly tasty," he said. And he started singing a little song:

F C G7 C
Stone Soup is what you need When you have some friends to feed
F C G7 G7 C
Step right up with what you got Add your STONES! to the big soup pot!

When the water came to a boil, the soldier tasted the soup.

"Mmmm!" he said.

"Is it ready?" asked the children.

"Not quite yet," said the soldier. "It needs a little salt."

"Ridiculous!" shouted the grown-ups.

But the blacksmith's brave little girl said, "We don't have much, but my family could spare a little salt."

"This is going to be an excellent Stone Soup," said the soldier. "But it would be even better with a bone or two."

"We don't have much," said the farmer's son, "but I know where I can get a few bones." And he ran home and came back with some.

All the children sang:

F
C
G7
C
Stone Soup is what you need When you have some friends to feed
F
C
G7
G7
C
Step right up with what you got Add your BONES! to the big soup pot!

"Mmmm!" said the soldier. "Delicious!"

"Is it ready?" asked the children.

"Not quite yet," said the soldier. "It needs a few onions or potatoes."

"My family has a few onions," said the washerwoman's son.
"And I can get some potatoes," said the mason's daughter.
F
C
G7
C
Stone Soup is what you need When you have some friends to feed

Each time the children asked if the soup was ready, the soldier would taste it and say, "Not quite yet. It would be even better with a few carrots. . . . It would be even better with a few beans. . . ."

The smell of the soup spread through the whole village. Even the grown-ups wanted a taste. The soldier knew he couldn't hold them off any longer.

He smacked his lips . . .

"It's the best Stone Soup ever!
Everybody get your bowls and spoons!"

“We made plenty,” smiled the children.

And the whole hungry village shared Stone Soup.

“I never thought stones
would taste so good.”

Thirty-five years ago, Pete first heard a version of "Stone Soup" told by his friend Jo Schwartz. Since then, Pete and his wife, Toshi, have been stirring things up (Stone Soup and chili) at the riverside festivals of *Clearwater*, a 106-foot sailing sloop that promotes environmental education and advocacy along the beautiful Hudson River. Year after year, the clean-river campaign has grown, with each new participant adding to the mix. Unbelievable—we can swim in the Hudson again. Stone Soup!

Some folks say the story of Stone Soup originated in Europe, but probably every culture has a version of its own. We've set our version in seventeenth-century Germany, where religious conflict led to the Thirty Years War (1616–1648). On one level, the story is about a soldier saved by his own wits. On another level, it's about how ordinary people deal with trouble, and the miraculous things that happen when people work together. Each person contributes some small part of the soup, and they end up with more than they thought they had. By joining together, what at first seems impossible becomes a meal for the whole village.

You might find examples of "Stone Soup" in your neighborhood. A community-built playground? One person has the tire. One person has the wood. Another has a long chain. Another has the tools. Then one day, everyone comes together, and before you know it, there's a wonderful playground.

The world is a big stone; it's what we bring to it that counts.

—Pete, Paul, & Michael